GIRLS ROCK!

Dog on the Loose

Holly Smith Dinbergs

illustrated by
Chantal Stewart

First Published in Great Britain by
RISING STARS UK LTD 2006
22 Grafton Street, London, W1S 4EX

For more information visit our website at:
www.risingstars-uk.com

British Library Cataloguing in Publication Data
A CIP record for this book is available from the British Library.

ISBN: 978-1-84680-063-4

First published in 2006 by
MACMILLAN EDUCATION AUSTRALIA PTY LTD
627 Chapel Street, South Yarra 3141

Visit our website at www.macmillan.com.au or go directly to
www.macmillanlibrary.com.au

Associated companies and representatives throughout the world.

Series created by Felice Arena and Phil Kettle
Project management by Limelight Press Pty Ltd
Cover and text design by Lore Foye
Illustrations by Chantal Stewart
Printed in China

UK Editorial by Westcote Computing Editorial Services

GIRLS ROCK!
Contents

Jess   *Sophie*

CHAPTER 1

Out for a Walk

Sophie and Jess are fast asleep on the floor of Jess's bedroom. Jess's cocker spaniel puppy, Sammy, comes up to Jess and licks her face.

Jess (yawning) "Sammy, I'm trying to sleep!"

With half-open eyes, Jess pats Sammy's neck and glances at the lump lying beside her.

Jess "You awake, Sophie?"
Sophie (mumbling) "Kind of."

Sophie pushes down the top of the sleeping bag.

Sophie "Hey, I totally forgot where I was. I thought I was camping out in a tent like we did last summer."

Jess "Only this is better. We didn't get wet and the toilet is just down the hall."

Sophie (laughing) "Yes, and we get to sneak into the kitchen and raid the bickie tin."

As Sophie stretches, the puppy walks over and sniffs her head.

Sophie (giggling) "Sammy, stop licking me. That tickles!"

Jess "He never gives up! Sammy, leave Sophie alone."

Sophie "I wish I could have more pets but Dad says I'm only allowed to have a cat."

Jess "But you're lucky. Puffles is so cute."

Sophie "Yes, but your room's like a zoo. Except that it doesn't stink."

In her room, Jess has three goldfish, two hermit crabs and a budgie.

Jess "I'm starving."

Sophie "Then let's eat."

Jess "OK, but Sammy really wants to go outside so we'll have breakfast after his walk. Do you want to come?"

Sophie "Of course. Race you!"

The girls get dressed and go to the utility room with Sammy close behind.

Jess "Here, boy. Let me put your lead on."

As Jess stuffs a plastic bag in her pocket, Sophie sees a note on top of the washing machine.

Sophie "Hey, there's a note from your Mum."

Jess "What does it say?"

Sophie "She's gone shopping and your Dad's next door."

Jess "It's OK. We'll be back before them."

Sammy yanks the girls out the door.

CHAPTER 2

That Confounded Cat

Jess and Sophie walk across the garden with Sammy and into the street. Sammy starts to sniff the ground.

Sophie "He can smell something."
Jess "He's looking for the right spot."
Sophie "The right spot? Like where somebody dropped a cheeseburger?"

Jess "No, where he can go … you know!"

Sophie "Oh yes. Cats are different. They just go in the garden or a litter tray."

The girls wait as Sammy goes. A few seconds later, Jess takes the bag out of her pocket to clean up the poo.

Jess "Here, hold the lead for a second."

Sophie "Isn't that gross? Cleaning up poo like that?"

Jess "No, not when it's your own
dog. And, see? I'm not actually
touching anything."

Sophie "No, and I suppose it's better
than leaving a mess on the street
for someone to step in."

While Jess is cleaning up, a huge
ginger cat jumps off the fence in front
of them and hisses at Sammy.

The cat races off and Sammy follows,
jerking the lead out of Sophie's hand.
As Sammy disappears around a
corner, the girls shout out.

Jess "Sammy, come back!
SAAAM-MEEEE!!"
Sophie "SAAAM-MEEEE!"

Sophie "Won't he come if you call?"

Jess "Sometimes, but he's only a puppy and he's still learning."

Sophie "I suppose a runaway cat doesn't help much either."

Jess "Mum's just starting to teach him all that stuff. Come on. We have to find him."

The girls run down the street in
search of Sammy, shouting out his
name as they go.

Jess "SAAAM-MEEEE. Come here,
boy."

Sophie "He has got to be round here
somewhere. He was here only a
minute ago so he can't have gone
very far."

CHAPTER 3

Squeak in the Park

The girls race around the corner only to find an empty street.

Jess "I can't see him down here."

Sophie "No, he must have kept going."

Jess "Oh no! We'll never find him. He's gone."

Sophie "It's all my fault. What if ..."

Jess "What if what?"

Sophie "What if there's a storm? He's just a puppy. He'll probably be afraid of thunder. I've heard that lots of dogs are afraid of thunder."

Jess "Sophie, see that big yellow thing in the sky? It's called the Sun. I don't think it's about to rain."

Sophie "I hope not. But how will Sammy find his way home?"

Jess "That's what worries me."

Sophie "I wish we could sprout wings. Then we could fly around and find him."

Jess "As if. I know! Sammy always comes running to play when I squeeze his squeaky mouse. And we always go to the park together, so perhaps he'll go there."

Sophie (excitedly) "Good thinking! He's probably at the park. Let's go."

Jess "But we have to go home first and get the squeaky mouse. I'm sure it'll help."

The girls go back to Jess's house and get the mouse. On the way to the park, they shout Sammy's name and squeeze the plastic toy. *Squeak!*

Jess "Sammy! Come here boy."
Sophie "Sammy! Come here."

At the park, the girls see some kids and dogs but no sign of Sammy.

Sophie (disappointed) "What if he's been kidnapped?"

Jess "What do you mean? Men in masks stealing my dog? That's more like dognapping!"

Sophie "Don't joke about it! I feel terrible. This is all my fault."

Jess "Don't worry, Sophie. We're going to find him. We just need some help."

Sophie and Jess ask some kids playing in the park to help find Sammy. Soon, they are all walking around calling Sammy's name. Meanwhile, Jess notices a poster on the fence.

Jess "Sophie, I know what we can do to find him."

CHAPTER 4

Posters, Please

The girls run back to Jess's house, squeezing the mouse and calling Sammy's name.

Jess "I'll get some paper and marker pens. We're going to make posters."

Sophie "Good idea!"

Jess disappears for a minute, then returns with the paper and pens.

Jess "What should we write?"
Sophie "How about 'Have you seen this dog?' in really big letters."

They each write the words on their paper.

Jess "We need to give a reward."

Sophie "But how much can we pay?"

Jess "I don't know. How much do you have?"

Sophie "I've got six pounds and thirteen pence."

Jess "I have about four pounds fifty."

Sophie "Let's just write 'Reward' and not say how much."

Jess "Cool."

Jess "What else should we write?"

Sophie "We need a picture of
Sammy. Have you got a photo
of him?"

Jess "No, we'll have to draw him."

Each girl draws a picture of
Sammy. Sophie shows hers to Jess.

Jess "That's not Sammy. That's an alien dog. Here, look at mine, it's better."

Sophie "Er … sorry, but that looks like a dark blob with eyes."

Jess "Is this really going to help, this poster idea? I'm getting worried. He'll be really scared by now. He's just a puppy."

Sophie "We need a real picture, not a drawing."

The girls hear a car door shut.

Jess "Mum's home. She'll probably be angry with us for losing Sammy, but she'll know what to do."

Just then, there's a knock on the back door.

CHAPTER 5

Home Sweet Home

Jess hears a bark. The girls look outside and see Sammy.

Jess "It's Sammy! He's home!"
Sophie "And it's the kids from the park. They must have found him!"

Jess flings open the door. She
picks up her puppy and gives him a
huge hug, while he excitedly tries to
lick her.

Sophie "Sammy, you're back! I'm so
glad you found him."
Jess "Thanks so much. You're stars!
I'm so pleased that Sammy's home
again."

The girls say goodbye to their friends and take Sammy inside. Jess finds her Mum putting away the groceries in the kitchen.

Jess "Mum, you'll never guess what happened."

Sophie "I think she probably knows. We left the posters out, remember?"

Jess "We took Sammy out while you were at the shops and he saw this cat and got really excited and before we knew it he'd run off and ..."

Sophie "Well, we thought we'd lost him forever but these kids at the park found him and brought him home."

Jess "He's had a scary morning, Mum. Can he have a treat?"

Jess's Mum pulls out a bag of doggy treats.

Jess "Hey Sophie, watch this! Sammy, sit. Now shake."

Sammy sticks his paw out, which Jess shakes. Jess gives the puppy his treat and pats his neck.

Jess "You are so good!"

Sophie "What a clever puppy!"

Jess eyes up the shopping as her Mum unpacks it.

Jess "Mum, I'm starving. We're really ready for breakfast. What do you want to eat, Sophie?"

Sophie "I really don't mind, as long as it's not dog biscuits!"

GiRLS ROCK!
Dog Lingo

Jess

Sophie

breed A kind of dog, for example, a cocker spaniel or a collie.

dog show A beauty contest for dogs.

dog tag ID for your dog. It is a small bit of plastic or metal you attach to your pet's collar that has all the important info about her, in case she gets lost.

labradoodle A cross between a labrador and a poodle.

poop scoop A little shovel used to clean up dog poo.

veterinary surgeon A doctor for animals.

GIRLS ROCK!
Dog Must-dos

☆ Be a responsible dog owner by making sure your dog is well trained, well fed, exercised regularly, clean and loved.

☆ Get a good book that tells you how to care for dogs.

☆ Brush your dog's teeth with special dog toothpaste (not human toothpaste) on a regular basis. That way your dog's breath will smell as sweet as roses!

☆ Take poo bags whenever you take your dog for a walk—nobody wants to step in dog dirt!

☆ Before patting a dog you don't know, ask for permission from its owner.

☆ If someone makes fun of you while you pick up dog poo, say "Do you like to step in dog poo?" or "All part of the service!"

☆ Take an obedience-training course with your puppy as soon as the vet says it's OK. With early training, your dog won't do crazy things that make people upset!

☆ Take your dog for regular walks and play with it as much as you can. Dogs who are bored or need attention often misbehave (just like people)!

Dog Instant Info

There are hundreds of different dog breeds (kinds of dogs).

Dogs' sense of smell and hearing are their most developed senses— and they smell and hear far better than humans. They can even sense earthquakes, sometimes.

Certain human foods are really bad for dogs. Chocolate, raisins or grapes can make dogs sick or even kill them.

The world record for the dog who can perform the most tricks goes to Chanda-Leah, a toy poodle, who can perform 469 tricks. She can play the piano, fetch a tissue if you sneeze and untie the knot in your shoelace.

A greyhound won the world record for the Dog High Jump by clearing a height of 167.6 centimetres in 2003.

The record for the world's shortest dog is currently held by a Yorkshire terrier named Whitney. From floor to shoulder, Whitney measures only 7.6 centimetres!

The world record for the largest litter of puppies is shared by three dogs. Each dog gave birth to 23 puppies— an American foxhound in 1944, a St. Bernard in 1975 and a Great Dane in 1987.

GIRLS ROCK!
Think Tank

1 What two senses are better in dogs than in humans?

2 What two dogs are crossed to create a labradoodle?

3 Name one of the tricks the world's trickiest dog can perform.

4 What do you do if your dog gets sick or is hurt?

5 How do you pick up dog dirt?

6 Where can your dog win a prize for being beautiful and well trained?

7 How do you help your dog to be found if it gets lost?

8 What kind of dog is best?

Answers

How did you score?

• If you got all 8 answers correct, you're probably already planning to go to veterinary school!

• If you got 6 answers correct, think about becoming a professional dog walker to make pocket money after school.

• If you got fewer than 4 answers correct, ask your Mum to buy you a goldfish or a bird for a pet!

Hey Girls!

I love to read and hope you do too! The first book I really loved was a book called "Mary Poppins". It was full of magic (way before Harry Potter) and I got hooked on reading. I went to the library every Saturday and left with a pile of books so heavy I could hardly carry them!

Here are some ideas about how you can make "Dog on the Loose" even more fun. At school, you and your friends can be actors and put on this story as a play. To bring the story to life, bring in some props from home such as a stuffed dog to be Sammy or a toy that squeaks when you squeeze it. Maybe you can set up a small table with pens and white paper for the poster scene.

Who will be Sophie? Who will be Jess? Who will be the narrator? (That's the person who reads the parts between Sophie or Jess saying something.) Once you've decided on these details, you're ready to act out the story in front of the class. I bet everyone will clap when you are finished. Hey, a talent scout from a television channel might just be watching!

See if somebody at home will read this story out loud with you. Reading at home is important and a lot of fun as well.

You know what my Dad used to tell me? "Readers are leaders!"

And remember, Girls Rock!

Holly Smith Dunberg

GIRLS ROCK!
When We Were Kids

Holly — Jacqueline

Holly talked to Jacqueline, another *Girls Rock!* author.

Jacqueline "Did you ever have a dog?"

Holly "When I was really little, I had a French poodle named Pierre. Later, I had two cocker spaniels, Sammy and Victoria, or Vickie for short."

Jacqueline "Did you ever enter your dogs in a dog show?"

Holly "No. They didn't sit or stay where they were supposed to."

Jacqueline "So they couldn't have won any prizes for 'most obedient dog'?"

Holly "No, but I should have won a prize for 'most poop scooped'!"

GIRLS ROCK!
What a Laugh!

Q What do you call a dog who loves bubble baths?

A A shampoodle!

GIRLS ROCK!

The Sleepover

Pool Pals

Bowling Buddies

Girl Pirates

Netball Showdown

School Play Stars

Diary Disaster

Horsing Around

Newspaper Scoop

Snowball Attack

Dog on the Loose

Escalator Escapade

Cooking Catastrophe

Talent Quest

Wild Ride

Camping Chaos

Mummy Mania

Skater Chicks